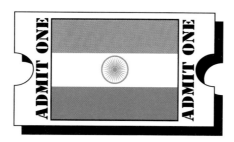

Taj Mahal
In Agra

# FACES AND PLACES

# INDIA

BY PATRICK RYAN

THE CHILD'S WORLD®, INC.

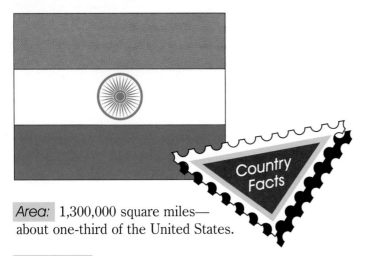

*Area:* 1,300,000 square miles— about one-third of the United States.

*Population:* About 950 million people.

*Capital City:* New Delhi.

*Other Important Cities:* Bombay, Calcutta, Madras.

*Money:* The rupee.

*National Language:* Hindi. Many other languages are also spoken in India, including English.

*National Song:* "Jana–gana–mana," or "Thou Art the Ruler of the Minds of All People."

*National Holiday:* Independence Day on August 15.

*National Flag:* Three stripes of orange, white and green. In the middle of the white stripe, there is a blue wheel. The wheel stands for the laws people follow in their lives.

*Heads of Government:* The president and the prime minister of India.

Text copyright © 1999 by The Child's World®, Inc.
All rights reserved. No part of this book may be reproduced or utilized in any form or by any means without written permission from the publisher.
Printed in the United States of America.

Library of Congress Cataloging-in-Publication Data
Ryan, Pat (Patrick M.)
India / by Patrick Ryan
Series: "Faces and Places".
p. cm.
Includes index.
Summary: Introduces the history, geography, people, and customs of the Asian nation of India.
ISBN 1-56766-579-9 (library : reinforced : alk. paper)

1. India — Juvenile literature.
[1. India] I. Title.

DS407.R92 1999
954 — dc21
98-44245
CIP
AC

**GRAPHIC DESIGN**
Robert A. Honey, Seattle

**PHOTO RESEARCH**
James R. Rothaus / James R. Rothaus & Associates

**ELECTRONIC PRE–PRESS PRODUCTION**
Robert E. Bonaker / Graphic Design & Consulting Co.

**PHOTOGRAPHY**
Cover photo: Rabari Girl at Name Giving Festival
by Tiziana and Gianni Baldizzone/Corbis

Table of Contents

Where Is India?

ADMIT ONE

ADMIT ONE

**I**magine looking at Earth from the moon. Most of what you see would be the blue oceans. The large areas of brown are called **continents**. There are seven of them. India is a triangle-shaped country that lies on the bottom of the continent of Asia. India is bordered on two sides by the Indian Ocean.

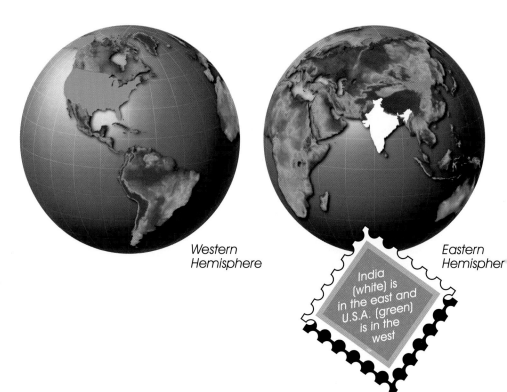

*Western Hemisphere*

*Eastern Hemispher*

India (white) is in the east and U.S.A. (green) is in the west

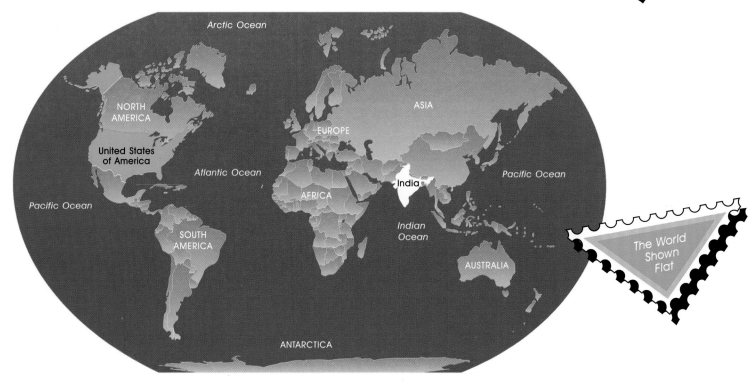

Arctic Ocean

NORTH AMERICA

United States of America

Atlantic Ocean

EUROPE

ASIA

AFRICA

India

Pacific Ocean

Pacific Ocean

SOUTH AMERICA

Indian Ocean

AUSTRALIA

ANTARCTICA

The World Shown Flat

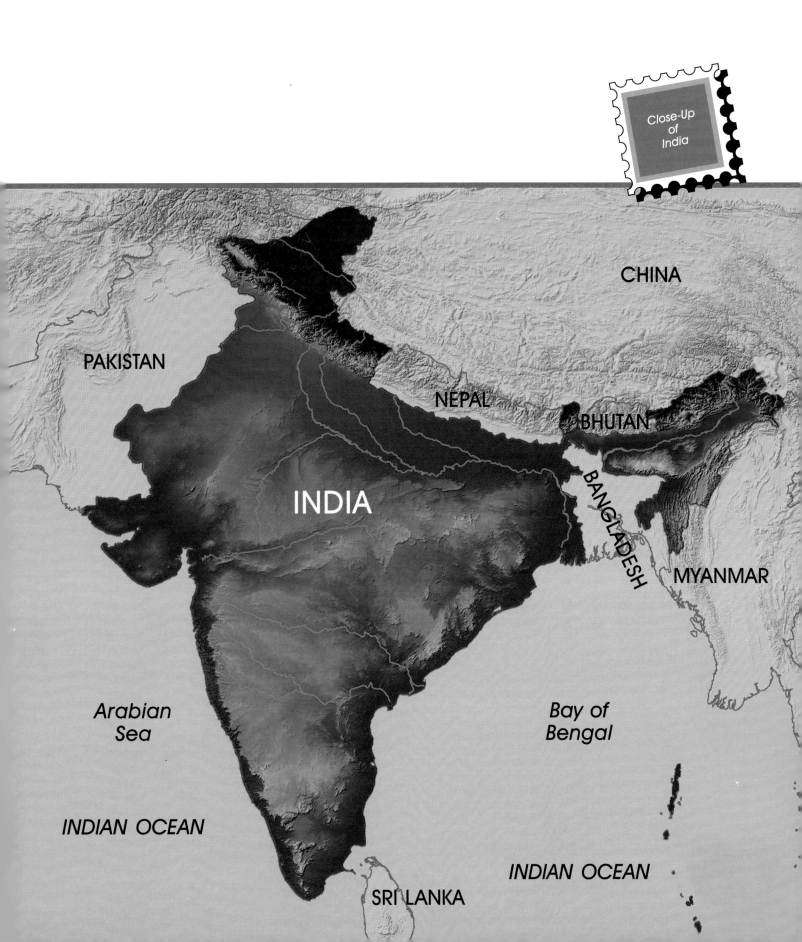

CHINA

PAKISTAN

NEPAL

BHUTAN

INDIA

BANGLADESH

MYANMAR

Arabian
Sea

Bay of
Bengal

INDIAN OCEAN

INDIAN OCEAN

SRI LANKA

Mountain
And
Terraced
Fields
In Sikkim

JAMMU &
KASHMIR
HIMALAYAS
Ganges
River •Agra
Benares•
SIKKIM
DECCAN
PLATEAU
•Mysore

David Samuel Robbins/Corbis

# The Land

Lalitha Mahal Sits On Deccan Plateau Near Mysore

**I**ndia is the seventh largest country in the world. Since it is so big, there are three different land areas. The area in the southern part of the country is called the Deccan Plateau. A **plateau** is a land area that is higher than the areas of land around it. The Deccan plateau is covered with flat plains.

The most important river in India is the *Ganges*. It brings water to people, plants and animals. It also is thought to have special powers. Along the Ganges, rich farmland can be found. There are rolling hills and plains here, too. The northern part of India is covered with tall mountains called the *Himalayas*. The Himalayas are the largest mountains in the world. Himalaya means " home of the snows".

Himalaya Mountains In Jammu & Kashmir

The Ganges River At Benares

# Plants & Animals

India is a land full of strange and beautiful animals. In fact, some people say that India is like a zoo from north to south! In India's thick jungles, snakes, elephants, and tigers live. Snow leopards make their homes high in the Himalayas. Wolves, bears, rhinos, and wild buffaloes can be found in many areas of India, too. There are more than 500 species of mammals and more than 2,000 different kinds of birds that live in India.

India's plant life is as varied as its animal life. In the north, trees such as evergreen, oak and cedar grow. Bamboo and palm trees grow tall and thick in the steamy jungles. Flowers and grasses of all kinds can also be found in India.

A Painted Elephant From Kanchipuram

Lindsay Hebberd/Corbis

Bengal Tiger In Ranthambhor National Park

Tom Brakefield/Corbis

Palm Trees On The Kerala Coast

Hans Georg Roth/Corbis

Joe McDonald/Corbis

HIMALAYAS

RANTHAMBHOR
NATIONAL PARK

ANDHRA
PRADESH

KERALA

• Kanchipuram

A Cobra
From
Andhra
Pradesh

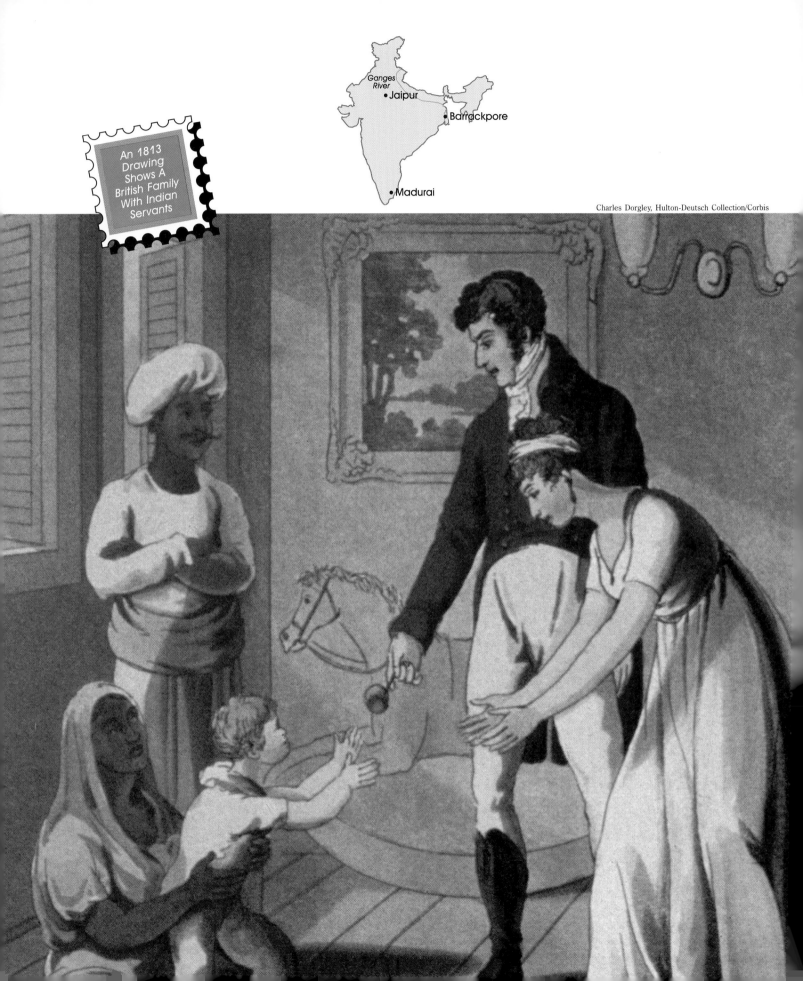

An 1813
Drawing
Shows A
British Family
With Indian
Servants

Ganges
River
• Jaipur
• Barrackpore

• Madurai

Charles Dorgley, Hulton-Deutsch Collection/Corbis

Ancient Palace Of The Winds, In Jaipur

Craig Lovell/Corbis

**P**eople have been living in India for thousands of years. The *Aryans* were one of the first groups of people to live in India. They divided themselves into different groups called **castes** (KASTS). In the caste system, people were born into jobs. If a child's father was a farmer, then the child would grow up to be a farmer, too.

For hundreds of years, India was made up of little kingdoms with their own rulers. Then people from other countries took over the kingdoms. They made new rules for India's kingdoms and created new laws. The last country to rule India was Great Britain.

Lower Caste Women Carry Food To Workers Near Madurai

1800's, Pagodas And Steps To River At Barrackpore

G. Hunt, Historical Picture Archive/Corbis

Enzo Ragazzini/Corbis

About 50 years ago, the people of India rose up. They did not want another country making laws for them. They wanted their own government with its own ideas. Many fights broke out between the British and Indian people. Great Britain did not want to give India up.

Then a peaceful man named Mahatma Gandhi spoke up. He wanted the fighting to stop. He used acts of non-violence to make the British people understand that India should be free. In 1947, Great Britain gave the government back to the people of India. Today, the people of India make their own laws to keep their people safe and happy.

The State Government Building In Bangalore

Robert Holmes/Corbis

Delhi's Presidential Palace

Jeremy Horner/©Corbis

Mahatma Gandhi With Grand-daughters In New Delhi

UPI/Corbis-Bettmann

Yann Arthus-Bertrand/Corbis

Delhi
☆
New Delhi

• Bangalore

Indian
Cavalrymen In
Dress Uniform,
1990-1997

Amritsar • HIMACHAL PRADESH
PUNJAB

• Pushkar

Hindu
Pilgrims
Come To
Bathe In
Pushkar Lake

Brian Vikander/Corbis

# The People

India has the second largest population in the world—about 950 million people. Only the country of China has more people. Most of India's people are relatives of the Aryans or other groups that came to India long ago.

Bennett Dean; Eye Ubiquitous/Corbis

Sikh Pilgrim At Golden Temple In Amritsar

India's people work hard. They also like to spend time with their families and friends. Religion is also very important to many Indians. In fact, many of India's holidays are religious celebrations.

Buddhist Pilgrims At A Ceremonial Rock In Himachal Pradesh

Arvind Garg/Corbis

Muslim Women At A Temple In Punjab

David Samuel Robbins/Corbis

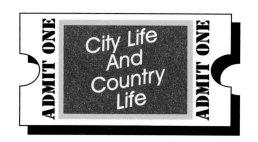

City Life
And
Country
Life

With so many people, India's cities are very crowded. Everywhere you look, there are people walking and talking. The bigger cities are full of busy streets and big buildings. There are shops and banks. There are hotels and restaurants, too. Most city dwellers live in tall apartment buildings.

Enzo Ragazzini/Corbis

Apartments And Busy Streets In Benares

Most of India's country people are farmers. They often live in small farming villages, in houses made from bricks or mud. In many of the houses, the only piece of furniture is a bed. During the day, they store the bed away so there is more room to cook and do chores.

Mud And Brick House In Ladakh

Bennett Dean; Eye Ubiquitous/Corbis

Hillside Houses in Darjeeling

Ric Ergenbright/Corbis

Zen Icknow/Corbis

LADAKH

•Jodhpur
Benares• •Darjeeling

Blue Houses
Crowded
Together
In Jodhpur

Playground
And School
Near
Gangtok

LADAKH

RAJASTHAN  Gangtok

Bombay

Jeremy Horner/©Corbis

# Schools And Language

India is a land of many languages—more than 200 are spoken throughout the country! The most common language is *Hindi*. English is also used as a common language by business people and government officials.

In schools, children are taught many of India's languages. They are also taught math, science and the arts. Students are hard-working and like to learn. If they study hard, Indian children can attend one of the country's fine colleges when they are older.

Charles & Josette Lenars/Corbis

Bombay University Tower Is British Design

Brian Vikander/Corbis

Teacher Moved Class Outside In Rajasthan

Outdoor Classroom In Ladakh

Earl Kowall/Corbis

# Work

Most of India's people work in the **trade** business. In this job, people grow crops or make things to sell to other countries. Cotton, peanuts, rice, and cheese are all things that Indians produce for the trade business. Wheat, milk, sugar cane and rubber are important trade products, too. India is also becoming known for its scientists. New discoveries in medicine, electronics, and computers are being made every day in India.

**Tourism** is another important job in India. In this job, Indians show visitors from other places about their country. Every year, many people come to India to see its fascinating sights. One of the most famous tourist attractions is the *Taj Mahal*. It is a huge, beautiful building that was built more than 300 years ago by a man named Shah Jahan.

Tourists Are Guided To The Taj Mahal In Agra

Sheldan Collins/Corbis

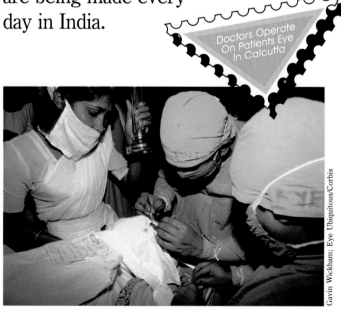

Doctors Operate On Patients Eye In Calcutta

Gavin Wickham; Eye Ubiquitous/Corbis

Men Clearing Nets Near Cochin

Jeremy Horner/©Corbis

Ganges River • Agra

Calcutta
Ganges Delta

• Cochin

Caroline Penn/Corbis

Farmer Plows Field For Rice Near Ganges Delta

Fancy Table
Setting In
Srinagar

Srinagar

SIKKIM

Kotagiri

Robert Holmes/Corbis

# Food

Indian people love spicy food. The most popular flavoring is a spice called *curry*. People will use curry to flavor almost everything—from salads to soup. Most Indians are **vegetarians**, which means they do not eat meat. Instead, they like to dine on lots of fruits and vegetables. Indians also like to eat dishes made with wheat and rice.

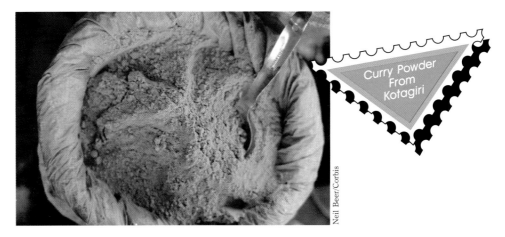

Curry Powder From Kotagiri

Neil Beer/Corbis

Some Indian meals are so spicy, they are served with a drink called *lassi*. Lassi is mixture of yogurt and water. Indians also drink a dark tea called *chai*.

Women Fetching Water For Meals

Snack Stand In Sikkim

Nazima Kowall/Corbis

Caroline Penn/Corbis

# Pastimes

Indian people love to go to movies. In fact, many large cities in India have hundreds of movie theaters! Indian people watch more movies than any other country. But the movie stars are not usually from Hollywood. Instead, India has its own stars.

Since Great Britain ruled India for so many years, many of the sports that are popular in India are also popular British pastimes. Soccer, tennis and field hockey are all favorite sports in India. *Cricket* is also popular with the Indian people. It is a game that is a little like baseball.

Catherine Karnow/Corbis

Cricket Team At Churchgate Station, Bombay

Boaters Relax On A River In Arunachal Pradesh

Tiziana and Gianni Baldizzone/Corbis

Movie Billboard In Jaipur

Geoffrey Taunton; Cordaiy Photo Library Ltd./Corbis

दिलवाले दुल्हनिया ले जायेंगे

RUPSHU

ARUNACHAL PRADESH

Jaipur

Bombay

Backpackers
Escape To
Rupshu Trek
For Peace
And Quiet

Hindus
Celebrating
Holi
Festival

New Delhi ☆
Agra
Darjeeling

Lindsay Hebberd/Corbis

Holidays
ADMIT ONE   ADMIT ONE

Holiday Visitors Leaving The Taj Mahal In Agra

Jeremy Horner/©Corbis

Lots of holidays and festivals are celebrated in India. Since religion is an important part of India, many of the celebrations are religious. *Holi* is a celebration to mark the end of the cold season. *Diwali* is India's "Festival of Lights." *Baisaki* is the New Year celebration for India's Hindu religion. *Ramadan* is a holiday for the Muslim religion. Some Indians celebrate Christmas and Easter, just like many Americans.

Maybe one day you will get a chance to visit India. If you did, you would find it to be a very interesting country. You could enjoy one of the celebrations, see the Taj Mahal, try some spicy food, or even see an Indian movie. There are many different things to see and do in India!

Darjeeling Children Celebrate Diwali With Sparklers

Earl Kowall/Corbis

Lindsay Hebberd/Corbis

Women Dancing For Republic Day In New Delhi

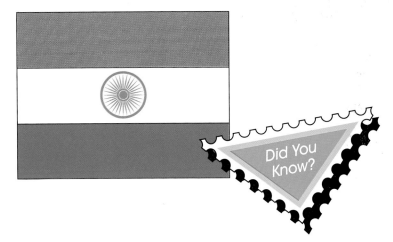

People who follow India's Hindu religion believe that no living creature should be hurt. Cows are thought to be very special animals. Instead of keeping them on farms, people let their cows go wherever they want to—even down city streets!

*Yoga* originally came from India. Yoga is a series of breathing exercises and body positions that help people relax.

With so many people in India, there are many who are poor and sick. In recent years, people have begun to help them. Mother Teresa was a woman who worked hard for India's poor. She cleaned them, fed them, and even stayed with them when they were dying. Today, other people carry on Mother Teresa's mission of caring.

India is the land of **monsoons**. Monsoons are ocean winds that often cause heavy rainfalls. The time of year when monsoons blow in is called the "rainy season." It begins in June and lasts several months. During one rainy season, an area of India can get up to 125 inches of rain.

How Do You Say?

|  | HINDI | HOW TO SAY IT |
| --- | --- | --- |
| Hello | namaste | (nah–MAH–stay) |
| Goodbye | namaste | (nah–MAH–stay) |
| Please | kripaya | (kri–pah–yah) |
| Thank You | dhanyavad | (dee–han–yah–vid) |
| One | ak | (ak) |
| Two | do | (do) |
| Three | tin | (tin) |
| India | Bharat | (bah–rot) |

## Glossary

**castes (KASTS)**
Castes are different groups of people. In the Indian caste system, children must grow up to do the same jobs their parents did.

**continent (KON–tih–nent)**
Most of the land areas on Earth are divided up into huge sections called continents. India is on the continent of Asia.

**monsoons (mon–SOONZ)**
Monsoons are ocean winds that often cause heavy rainfalls. Monsoon season lasts several months in India.

**plateau (pla–TOH)**
A plateau is an area of land that is higher than the land around it. The Deccan Plateau is a plateau in the southern part of India.

**tourism (TOOR–ih–zem)**
The business of showing travelers around a country is called tourism. Tourism is a growing business in India.

**trade (TRAYD)**
Growing crops or making things to sell to other countries is called the trade business. Many Indians work in the trade business.

**vegetarians (veh–jeh–TARE–ee–enz)**
Vegetarians are people who do not eat meat. Many Indians are vegetarians.

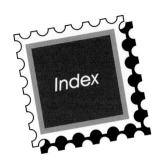

## Index